Mystery at Mockingbird Manor

by LAURIE PASCAL and JAMIE PASCAL

illustrated by DAVID PREBENNA

D1073346

SCHOLASTIC INC.
New York Toronto London Auckland Sydney

ISBN 0-590-32812-3

13 12 11 10 9 8 7 6 5 4 3 2   3 4 5 6 7 8 9/9

For our father, Jerry Offenberg

READ THIS FIRST

Are you ready for some really fantastic adventures?

Start reading on page 1 and keep going until you have to make a choice. Then decide what you want to do and turn to that page.

Keep going until you reach **THE END**. Then, you can go back and start again. Every path leads to a new story!

It is all up to you!

Wow! You can hardly believe it's true! But you are actually going to spend your winter vacation working at Mockingbird Manor, your grandfather's hotel high up in the Rocky Mountains. Just think— you can go skiing, mountain climbing, and swimming all in the same place!

You pack your favorite dress with the lace collar, your new shoes, and the rest of your best clothes. You figure there will be lots of parties and dinners because the hotel is very fancy.

Unfortunately, your mother reminds you that you will be working. She suggests that you pack your snow boots, jeans, and sweat shirts, too. Thanks, Mom!

Turn to **page 2.**

2   After three days of packing and re-packing, it's finally time to get on the plane. You're so excited you can't sit still. You feel like doing cartwheels in your seat!

After your plane lands, you ride a bus up to the hotel. It's fabulous! The building is more than one hundred years old. It looks like a giant cuckoo clock stuck right on top of a mountain. There are miles of pine trees all around, and you can see a shiny blue lake down below.

Your job is to help the desk clerk. That way, you can learn all about the hotel from top to bottom. Grandfather says that if you do a terrific job, one day he hopes to turn the whole place over to you!

Go on to the next page.

This week is going to be very exciting. **3**
Lots of famous people have checked into
Mockingbird Manor.

• The big rock star, fabulous Jimmy
Hitchcock, has a suite on the third floor.
Next to him there's a strange-looking
man who calls himself John Doe.

• Up on five is the beautiful movie
star, Lillian Safire.

• On the fourth floor, there's a well-
known detective.

• On the top floor is a man who is as
handsome as a prince in a storybook. In
fact, he *is* a prince—Prince Ali of Abba.
He has two bodyguards to keep everyone away—including you!

• On the second floor is the most
mysterious guest of all, Madame Grimaldi. She's a world-famous magician,
traveling with her husband.

An old friend of your grandfather's is
here too. His name is Hank Winters.
He's a famous rocket scientist.

Turn to **page 4.**

HANK WINTER

THE DETECTIVE

MADAME GRIMALDI

JOHN DOE

JIMMY HITCHCOCK

PRINCE ALI of ABBA

LIAN SAFIRE

Turn to **page 6.**

6   One morning, the desk clerk asks you to bring breakfast up to the actress, Lillian Safire. After that, you go over to Grandfather's office. It's in a small cabin behind the hotel.

To your surprise, the office is empty. How strange. Grandfather always spends the morning there. You are just about to leave when you notice a note pinned to the door—with a dagger!

If you want to see your grandfather again Don't tell anyone he's gone. We will contact you.

What should you do?

If you decide to look for your grandfather, turn to **page 7.**

If you wait for the kidnappers to contact you, turn to **page 21.**

You decide to look for your grandfather, but you must be very careful not to let anyone know he's missing. You squeeze your face into a big smile and walk out of the cabin.

You say "hi" to the gardener and admire his evergreen shrubs. You hope you can stop trembling!

When you reach the lobby of the hotel, you suddenly hear somebody call out your name. Slowly you turn around and find yourself facing—the detective!

Turn to **page 8.**

"I'm looking for your grandfather," he says. "Have you seen him this morning?"

You'd better think fast before you answer. "Uh, well," you stutter, "Grandfather always sleeps late on Saturday."

The detective looks surprised. "But this is Sunday," he says.

"Wow! Then I'd better wake him right now," you shout. Then you spin around and race off toward Grandfather's bedroom in the hotel.

Once inside, you lock the door behind you. *Whew!* Close call! It isn't long before you realize there is something wrong. What is that chef's hat doing on your grandfather's dresser?

Go on to the next page.

And there's a note in Grandfather's handwriting:

Do not serve the strawberry ice cream cake!

When you examine the dresser more closely, you see something else: There are numbers written in dust on the dresser—404. Is that a secret code or a room number? Should you check out Room 404 or rush to the kitchen to investigate the chef's hat—and the cake?

If you decide to go to Room 404,
turn to **page 11.**

If you decide to go to the kitchen,
turn to **page 14.**

10   The elevator keeps rising—with you standing on top of it! The prince must be going to the top floor! You start pushing buttons near the hatch. They look like emergency buttons, but nothing happens!

You're running out of time, and nothing seems to be working. "I'll lie down flat," you decide, hoping the elevator won't go all the way to the top floor.

But it is going—to the *very top!* You are going to be squished!

You squeeze your eyes tightly shut and scream. When you open your eyes again, you find your mother leaning over you, comforting you.

"You're having a bad dream," she tells you. Then you realize—you're not leaving for Grandfather's hotel until tomorrow! You're safe at home, in your own bed, in your own room. Thank goodness!

THE END

You dash up to Room 404. You remember that it's the room where Mr. Winters, the rocket scientist, is staying.

The room door is open a crack. You poke it open a little more, then just a little more, until, finally, you see something: It's a pair of legs with a rope wrapped around the ankles! Oh, oh! Maybe you should have stayed home! But it's too late for that. Very quietly, you enter the room and pull the door closed. Just before it's about to click, you realize that it could be your grandfather tied up in that chair!

You're scared to death, but you have to go over and see who it is.

Turn to **page 12.**

12   You walk over and hope with all your might that you've found Grandfather—alive! As you creep closer on your tip-toes, you see that it's Hank Winters! You untie him quickly and tell him about the dagger, the note, and your missing grandfather.

Mr. Winters thanks you for finding him. He explains that he has invented a new kind of rocket. He tells you that he gave the secret plans to your grand-father to hide for him just before a spy came and tied him up.

This is so complicated, you can hardly understand it! And then—all of a sud-den—a rock comes crashing through the window! It has a note wrapped around it. The note says:

MEET ME IN THE BASEMENT. COME ALONE.

Go on to the next page.

"You'd better go," Hank Winters says. "My knee is hurt. I can't even walk."

Should you do it? Or should you just keep searching for your grandfather?

*If you follow the instructions on the note
and go to the basement,
turn to* **page 24.**

*If you continue your search
for Grandfather,
turn to* **page 28.**

14   You go to the kitchen. Everything looks normal.

Just then you hear footsteps, and the chef comes in from the dining room. He's not wearing his hat, so you know he must have been in Grandfather's room.

The chef looks upset.

"What's the matter?" you ask.

"We ran out of desserts," the chef says. "There's nothing left but that strawberry ice cream cake your grandfather made for his friend Hank Winters. I'll have to serve that and make another cake for Mr. Winters later."

You remind the chef that Grandfather left orders not to serve the cake.

"I know," the chef says, "but this is an emergency."

Go on to the next page.

The chef reaches into the freezer and takes out the strawberry ice cream cake.

Something tells you you had better stop him. What should you do? Should you try to talk him out of serving the cake? Or should you just grab it out of his hands and run?

If you try to talk the chef out of serving the cake, turn to **page 52**.

If you grab the cake and run, turn to **page 16**.

16   You rush over to the chef and snatch the cake—carefully—out of his hands!

"Hey, what—" he mutters. You run to the door, but the chef is there first. He blocks the way.

"Drop that cake," he says. "I mean, hand over that cake! I must have it!" You are so scared that you hand the cake right over.

The chef puts the cake down on the counter. He takes a knife, slices the top off the cake, and reaches inside. To your surprise, he pulls out some papers.

Go on to the next page.

"Aha!" he says. "The secret plans for Hank Winters' new rocket. Winters gave them to your grandfather for safekeeping. Luckily for me, I saw where the old man put them. I know some people who will give me a lot of money for these plans."

While the chef is talking, your eyes fall on a big bowl of butter sitting on the counter. The chef starts to run out the door, but you grab the bowl and toss the butter under his feet. "You'll never get away with this," you yell.

The chef slips and slides on the butter. He hits his head against the counter and falls down, unconscious.

You take the papers out of his hands and race out of the kitchen. Now what should you do?

If you take the papers to the safe,
turn to **page 30.**

If you go for help,
turn to **page 54.**

You've ended up at the rock star's room. As you arrive you see that weird man, John Doe, running out holding a bunch of papers. Could they be the secret rocket plans?

You run after him, down the stairs and out through the lobby. As you pass the desk clerk, you yell out, "Call the Police!"

John Doe is running just ahead of you. When he sees you chasing him, he jumps onto the ski lift. He's getting away! Suddenly you have an idea—you let him ride the ski lift until he's halfway down the slope. Then you stop the lift.

Just a few feet away from you is a cabin full of ski equipment. Quickly you find a pair of boots and skis and put them on. Then you ski to where Mr. John Doe is dangling.

Go on to the next page.

"I'll let you down if you drop those papers," you tell him. He does, but then a big gust of wind blows them away! You begin to ski after them, but you see they are blowing toward the slippery glacier!

You look down. It's a long slide, but you've *got* to have those papers! You're scared because skiing is something you haven't done in a long time. But you still remember how! So here goes!

Turn to **page 20.**

20   You're off! The wind is blowing hard in your face, but it will be worth it to have those papers. You finally hit bottom and reach them. But when you start to read, you can't believe it. These papers are not the secret rocket plans—they are pages from the rock star's diary!

Boy, you're really trapped now. You can't get off this glacier by yourself. You hope the desk clerk called the police and that they will know where to look for you.

That John Doe must have been a sneaky gossip columnist! Oh, well, there's nothing to do but read these papers until the police come to get you.

What a shock! On the very first page you find that Jimmy Hitchcock, the famous rock star, still sleeps with his teddy bear!

THE END

You decide that the safest thing to do is to wait for the kidnappers to contact you. You wish they would hurry because you're so worried!

Your mother always told you the best way to make time go quickly is to keep busy. So, fighting back the tears, you tell yourself to have courage. Just deal with the problems of the day, and keep smiling.

Wouldn't you know it: There are *millions* of problems today. And *you* must solve them all.

For starters, the desk clerk tells you that fifteen campers have decided they want to sleep inside for a change. So you have the bellboys clear out the main ballroom for them, saying, "Grandfather's orders."

Turn to **page 22.**

22   Thank goodness, the campers don't mind sleeping on the floor.

Then you dash off to the room of Lillian Safire, the movie star, to find out why she's screaming at the bellboy and waking up all her napping neighbors.

"The sink on the floor above is leaking," she wails, "and water is dripping right into my cereal."

"Then just move your cereal," you tell her. And she does. She's very pleased at your solution!

"Funny lady," you giggle, as you go upstairs to check the leaking sink. Well, no wonder the sink's leaking: Someone put the plug in but forgot to turn off the faucet. You do it and feel very grown-up at your common-sense solutions.

Suddenly the elevator alarm goes off! At the front desk, the desk clerk tells you, "The prince is stuck in the elevator on the second floor!"

Go on to the next page.

You dash to the third floor, pull the elevator door open, and peek down to find the problem. The elevator rope is caught on a hook. You grab the rope, shimmy down to the second floor, and release it. It's a good thing you took rope climbing in gym!

But suddenly the elevator starts going up—and you're on top of it! You're going to be squished!

If you try to stop the elevator,
turn to **page 10.**

If you try to pry open the hatch,
turn to **page 38.**

24   You sneak down to the basement door. How dark it is down there!

It's so quiet that each step creaks. You're getting more and more nervous. You're almost at the bottom when you hear a voice calling your name.

It's Grandfather! He is holding a flashlight. You run toward him and hug and kiss him a million times. "I escaped from the kidnappers," he tells you, "and then I threw a rock in Hank's window and came here to hide. There are spies all over the place. Luckily, the rocket plans are safely hidden."

Grandfather asks you to wiggle through a secret tunnel down to his wine cellar and get the plans.

You do! It makes you feel like you're in a spy movie. Only this is really true.

"Good going!" Grandfather says, hugging you. Then you both wait in the basement until it gets very dark outside. You leave the basement and sneak out through a secret door.

Turn to **page 26.**

"We'll have to take my snowmobile," Grandfather says. The two of you race down the mountain as fast as you can. Then you stop at a private heliport. "Hop in," Grandfather tells you. Up, up you climb! You can see Mockingbird Manor down below as you fly over the mountain.

Go on to the next page.

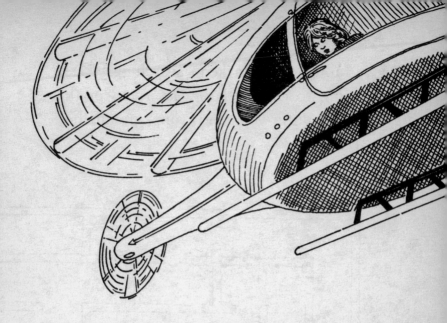

Finally, you arrive at FBI headquarters. It's the first time you've ever landed on a rooftop!

After you land, you hand the secret rocket papers over to the FBI. You are a hero!

THE END

28   You decide to keep searching. You're going to check *every last room* in this hotel until you find your grandfather. Here goes!

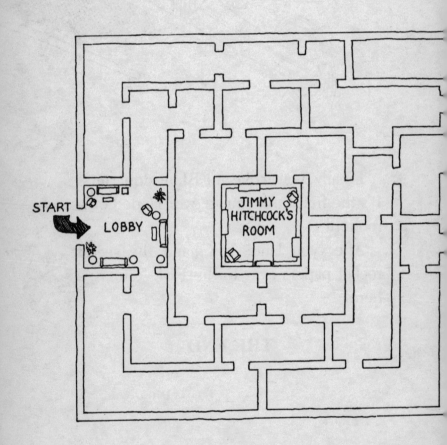

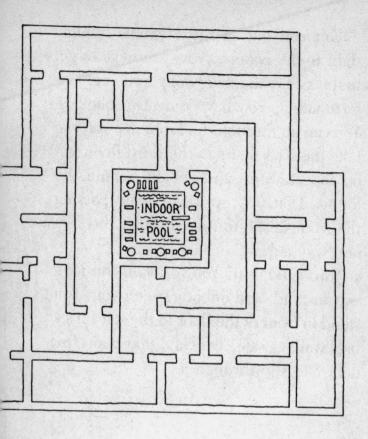

*If you've gone through the maze, and
ended up at the indoor pool,
turn to* **page 40.**

*If you've gone through the maze, and
ended up at the rock star's room,
turn to* **page 18.**

30   You run out of the kitchen, holding tight to the papers. Now you have to get to the safe without anybody noticing. Unfortunately, you have only two choices. You can go through the lobby, or you can take the back stairs to the third floor, get on the elevator, and get off behind the lobby. That way, you can avoid passing the front desk. You decide that the second way is best.

You've done it! You've taken the long way around, and nobody's seen you. You stand in front of the door to the safe. It's a big, walk-in safe. Quickly, you open the door and slip through it.

Go on to the next page.

Boom! The door slams shut! And you can't open it no matter how hard you try. You are trapped in a pitch black safe. What are you going to do now? "Why didn't I go through the lobby," you moan. "Then somebody would have seen me come in here."

Sadly, you remember what Grandfather once told you about the safe: There's only enough air in there for fourteen hours!

But maybe somebody *did* notice you. You hope so. Besides, someone is sure to open the safe sometime during the afternoon.

At least you have the papers safely with you. So you've saved the day.

Now, who will save **you?**

THE END

You hide in the closet just as the door is flung open and Madame Grimaldi walks in. She takes the suitcase with the paper in it and leaves. Grandfather doesn't even move. You call the police, telling them about Madame Grimaldi and the money.

In a few minutes the police call back. They've caught Madame Grimaldi at the airport. "Hooray!" you shout.

"What's this all about?" asks your Grandfather. He seems like himself again —the telephone ringing must have jolted him out of the spell.

After you explain the whole story to him, he says, "From now on, you are the personal tour guide for our newest guest, the famous actor and singer, Rick Rogers.

"Wow!" is all you can say to that!

THE END

You start telling Grandfather about the problems you've been having.

"Let's go and see if we can find out why the workers want to go on strike," Grandfather says. But just then, the door opens. You're trapped behind it! Before you can say, "ouch," you see someone's hand and hear the sound of fingers snapping. Grandfather stops in his tracks. He gets a funny, faraway look in his eyes.

Into the room steps Madame Grimaldi, the magician. Now you know what happened. Madame Grimaldi has just hypnotized your grandfather!

Turn to **page 34.**

34   *Oh, no,* you think, *this is like a scary mystery movie.* You can't seem to move or speak.

Madame Grimaldi marches right up to your grandfather and says something to him in a low voice. She must be giving him some kind of command, but you can't hear what it is. Then she spins around and leaves the room.

What should you do now?

If you follow Madame Grimaldi to see what she's up to, go on to the next page.

If you stay with your grandfather, turn to page 50.

You follow Madame Grimaldi, staying a safe distance behind so she won't notice you. She goes up to her room and, luckily, forgets to shut the door all the way. You sneak over and listen as you hear her begin to talk.

"I told the old man to pack the money," she says. "Now it's time to get out of here. I've got the deed to Mockingbird Manor that I made him sign, too. We're going to be *very* rich!"

"I've got to do something," you tell yourself. Unfortunately, you say it out loud and Madame Grimaldi hears you!

She rushes over, looks through the crack in the door, and then pulls you in by the back of your neck!

Turn to **page 36.**

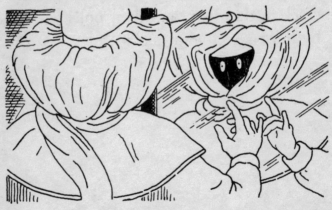

"I'll just have to hypnotize you, too, you little snoop," she says. She zeros in on you with her powerful eyes. You'd better think fast because she's staring at you *very* hard.

You notice that you are standing in front of a mirror—with no place to run. You try closing your eyes to get away from that hypnotic stare. Suddenly it's quiet. You look up and see something amazing: Madame Grimaldi seems to be frozen. Then you realize what's happened: She's hypnotized herself! The hypnotic spell bounced off the mirror and reflected back onto her!

Go on to the next page.

You call the police, and they take her and her husband into custody. Then you find the deed that she hypnotized your grandfather into signing, and you bring it back to him.

He's so relieved, he gives you the rest of the day off!

THE END

38   The elevator is moving pretty quickly, but you know that you can open the elevator hatch in an emergency.

So you try prying it open with your fingers. But there's not enough room for your fingers to squeeze through. Then you remember that you're wearing a belt and the buckle would probably be the perfect tool. You rip the buckle off as quickly as possible and—it works!

You fling the hatch open just in the nick of time. And guess where you land —in the prince's arms!

Go on to the next page.

"Are you all right?" he asks you. You feel like you are in a fairy tale—the part that is "happily ever after."

But the dream ends when the door opens. The prince thanks you over and over for rescuing him from the stuck elevator. Then he puts you down, and you dust yourself off.

Now you must get back to business and find Grandfather—or *wait* for the kidnappers to get in touch with you.

So, you head back toward Grandfather's office.

Turn to **page 43.**

40   Here you are at the indoor pool. This is the last place you can look. You are starting to get *very* nervous about Grandfather. You've racked your brains and, so far, no luck. Since this is probably the last place he can be, you hope with all your might that he *will* be here!

As you open the door and look around, you see nothing but a bunch of empty chairs surrounding an empty pool.

You check out the locker rooms—nothing. And the exercise room—still nothing.

You find yourself walking up and back by the pool, staring at it and thinking.

You've never been so unhappy in your life!

You can't imagine what's happened to Grandfather. "Maybe I'll just sit by the edge of the pool and think," you tell yourself. You do, and suddenly, someone sneaks up behind you and pushes you into the pool!

Go on to the next page.

"Uh-oh!" you think. "I'm in big trouble now—because I can't swim!" You start shouting, "HELP! HELP!"

You feel yourself sinking down down down. Then, from out of nowhere, you feel a strong arm around your neck. Someone is saving you! You have no idea who it is.

Turn to **page 42.**

42   When he pulls you out, you open your eyes and look up into his. Oh, goodness! It's the prince!

"Oh, thank you!" you blurt out.

"It was my pleasure," he says. You'd like to just stay here forever, but you remember that you've *got* to find your grandfather.

First, you'd better go to your room and dry off! You say good-bye to the prince and race up to your room. Quickly you change into dry clothes and comb your hair. Then you head for the dark, gloomy basement.

Turn to **page 24.**

You enter Grandfather's office and sit down in his favorite chair in the corner. When the phone rings, you pick it up quickly. It's the desk clerk, Harvey. He tells you that fifteen Japanese tourists have arrived without a reservation, and he has no place to put them. He also says that the staff is going to strike—everyone except him.

You tell him to calm down, and ask him to tell the Japanese tourists to check the hotel on the next mountain. Harvey sounds a little calmer. "And since I'm in charge of the hotel, now," you tell Harvey, "I order you to deal with the strike."

You hang up the phone quickly, wishing you were at home with your mother and father and your Barbie dolls!

Turn to **page 44.**

44   Just then, in walks Grandfather! You've never been so happy to see anyone in your whole life. Your smile is so big that your cheeks hurt.

You tell Grandfather about the dagger and the note, and he says that someone must have been playing a joke. He seems fine, and you're so relieved. Now you don't have to worry about the strike. Grandfather will take care of everything.

Go on to the next page.

Just then, you glance out the window, and see somebody looking in—a person wearing a parka and a ski mask. A very suspicious-looking character! Should you go and find out who that person is—or stay and help your grandfather?

If you decide to follow the person in the parka, turn to **page 46.**

If you decide to stay with Grandfather, turn to **page 33.**

46   You go out and look for the person in the parka and the ski mask. There he is— he's just about to get into his skis! You run inside and put on your ski clothes and boots as fast as you can. Outside again, you see the suspicious-looking skier heading for the trail that goes to the bottom of Mockingbird Mountain. You put on your skis and follow.

Go on to the next page.

It's cold as the wind hits your face, but it feels good! This is the fastest skiing you've ever done in your life!

The person in the ski mask is a very good skier, swerving neatly to avoid trees. You follow after and start yelling, "STOP! STOP! I HAVE TO TALK TO YOU!"

Turn to **page 48.**

48   At the bottom of the trail, the person in the ski mask just *has* to stop. You rush over to get a good look.

"It was great racing you!" the person says, and slips off the mask. Suddenly, long golden curls tumble down from underneath. It's Lillian Safire, the actress!

Go on to the next page.

"Why were you snooping around Grandfather's window?" you ask her.

"Oh," she starts laughing. "I wasn't snooping on you. I'm not supposed to be skiing because I'm starting a new movie tomorrow. My director is terrified that I'll break a leg or something! So I had to be sure he wasn't around to see me."

You laugh along with her, and then Lillian Safire says, "Want to race again?"

"Sure!" you say—and this time you beat her!

THE END

50   The door slams behind Madame Grimaldi, and Grandfather immediately walks over to the safe. He's moving around just like a robot! It's very weird. He seems to have forgotten that you are in the room.

Slowly, he opens the safe and begins taking out all his money and putting it into a suitcase. This is terrible! You're not sure what to do, and you don't have much time to waste.

"Grandfather!" you say. You snap your fingers and clap your hands in front of his face. "It's me!"

Go on to the next page.

But he pays absolutely no attention. It's as if you're not even in the room.

You must take action! You look around the room in a panic trying to think of some way to get the money and safely hide it before Madame Grimaldi comes back.

Grandfather finishes packing the money, closes the suitcase, and returns to his desk. He sits there staring straight ahead. Then you look around and notice another suitcase exactly like the one he put all the money into. You have a brilliant idea! You quietly take the second suitcase into the closet and stuff it with paper. Then you come back out and switch suitcases, putting the one with the money into the closet.

Turn to **page 32.**

52   The chef is about to step out the door with your grandfather's strawberry ice cream cake. "Wait," you call. "I'll take it out to the dining room for you."

"All right." The chef hands you the cake. "Be careful—don't drop it."

You run out the door with the cake and run right into the rock star, Jimmy Hitchcock.

"Hey," says Jimmy Hitchcock, "my favorite dessert—cherry ice cream cake." He reaches out to grab the cake away from you.

Go on to the next page.

"No," you say, pulling back. But Jimmy Hitchcock grabs at the cake platter, and it slips out of your hands— *splat!* You both stand looking down at the mess.

"It wasn't even cherry," you say. "It was strawberry."

"Oh, then everything's all right," he says. "I couldn't have eaten it. I'm allergic to strawberries." He goes off whistling.

Well, that clue didn't lead you anywhere. But you remember that mysterious number 404 traced in the dust on the dresser. You decide to go to Room 404 and see if you can find anything there.

Turn to **page 11.**

54   You take the papers and run to find the detective. He is in his room, thank goodness!

You tell the detective the whole story. He shakes his head. "I've been on the trail of that man for weeks," he says. "He's not a chef at all. He's a spy who sells secrets to enemy agents. We'd better get those plans to the safe—fast."

Just then the door opens and three strange men walk in.

"Oh-oh," the detective whispers to you. "Enemy agents."

The biggest man walks right up to you. "All right, kid," he says, "hand over those plans. If you do, we'll return your grandfather safe and sound. If you don't, you'll never see him again."

What can you do? You give the papers to the enemy agent. The three men hurry out the door.

Turn to **page 56.**

56   Two hours later, Grandfather walks in. You're so glad to see him! But you are also worried.

"What will happen now that the spies have the secret plans for the new rocket?" you ask.

Grandfather bursts out laughing. "They don't have the plans!" he says. "The papers you gave them were fakes. I knew there were spies all around, so I drew up the fake plans and put them in the cake. I made sure the spies saw me. In the meantime, the real plans were being delivered to Washington."

Go on to the next page.

Wow! You can hardly wait to tell your
friends about this exciting adventure.
But Grandfather tells you not to tell
anybody. It's supposed to be top secret.

Can you keep a secret? You don't
know, but you'll try.

THE END